THE GOOSE WHO KNEW TOO MUCH

Peter Utton

Hi! I'm Myrna. Read about our fight with nasty Mr Stalecrust.

A & C Black • London

The comix series ...

First published in paperback 2003. Reprinted 2004
First published in hardback 2002 by A & C Black Publishers Ltd
37 Soho Square, London W1D 3QZ
www.acblack.com

Text and illustrations copyright © 2002 Peter Utton

The right of Peter Utton to be identified as author
and illustrator of this work has been asserted by him in
accordance with the Copyrights, Designs and Patents Act 1988.

ISBN 0-7136-6177-1

A CIP catalogue record for this book is available from the
British Library.

A & C Black uses paper produced with elemental, chlorine-free pulp,
harvested from managed sustainable forests.

Printed and bound in Spain by G. Z. Printek, Bilbao

CHAPTER ONE

A wandering goose heard the sound of voices...

Good grief, Myrna, these cakes are like rocks!

Well if you think you can cook them better, you try it!

5

Really? Was it a blind man with a stick who looked exactly like me?

No, nothing like you. He had black hair and orange sidewhiskers.

And he wasn't too charming either!

The man looked anxious and he paced around the room.

Oh dear! That sounds like Mr Stalecrust. A rather nasty piece of work from the town. He's been trying to buy Galahad for some time now.

21

The amazing thing is, Galahad somehow knows who the winners will be at the local horse races! And the only person who understands what Galahad says is my brother Jed!

And sometimes, when we're a bit short of money, or we fancy a little holiday, Jed and I, with Galahad's help, will have a little flutter on the horses...

Myrna, let's get out of here! He's flipped... loopy... lost his marbles... barmy!

Stuart was not taking Joe, or his story, very seriously.

25

26

Help? What can we do?
We could watch the betting shop to see if old Stalecrust puts a bet on.
Good grief, Robert, that's a GOOD IDEA!
You wait here, Joe, and we'll report back to you.
Right you are, Myrna, and thank you so much!
You're not serious, Myrna. He's obviously barking mad!
I don't think he is. And his brother and Galahad are missing...
That's if he's got a blind twin brother!

27

CHAPTER FOUR

Mr Stalecrust had a small flat above a newsagent's.

Hmm...

They returned to Joe's cottage.

He can't be hiding Jed and Galahad in his flat, Joe, it's too tiny. People would know.

But if he looked angry then he obviously didn't win his bet!

Perhaps Galahad's been giving him false information.

29

...we could dress him up to look like Jed. Give him a stick and dark glasses.

What's the point of that, genius?

Then old Stalecrust sees him around town, and thinks Jed has escaped!

And then Stalecrust rushes back to where he's hiding them...

...and we follow him and he leads us to Jed and Galahad!

CHAPTER FIVE

Joe found a spare pair of dark glasses, a white stick and one of Jed's berets.

CHAPTER SIX

The very next day they saw the villain leaving the betting shop.

44

In the mill a confused Mr Stalecrust was checking a small, locked room.

46

48

49

OW! You're a proper devil and no mistake!
Here, how come you've had a shave? And you've changed your pullover!
It's the goose, you know. He's not only a fortune teller. He's a wizard as well!
He can also turn himself into a ferocious crust-eater!

59

CHAPTER SEVEN

Well, well, Jack, up to your old tricks again?

I'll confess to everything... anything! Just get me out of here!

We could say, you're coming 'clean', eh Jack? Ha, Ha!

They're all mad! Bonkers!

That goose isn't a real goose, sergeant. It's a wizard.

Of course it is, Jack.

62

63